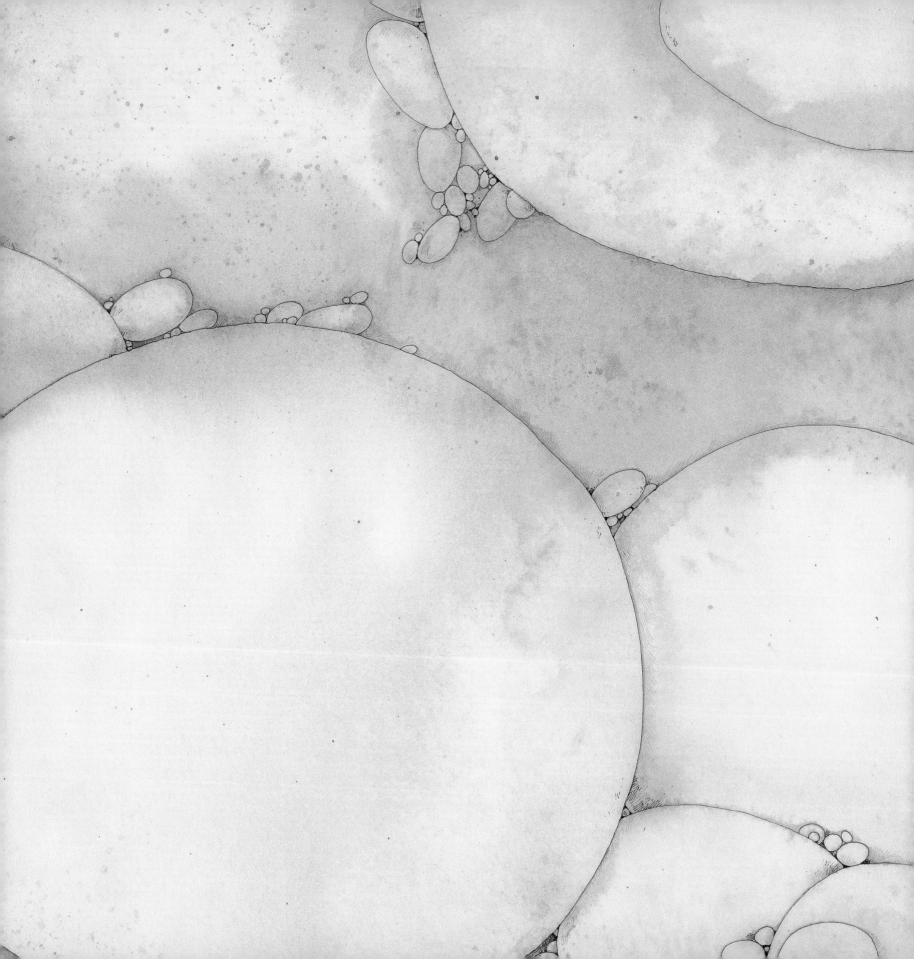

Wonderful Life

For the dreamers who find themselves travelling further and more hopefully—

and for Sheila - H.W.

A TEMPLAR BOOK

First published in the UK in 2007 by Templar Publishing,
an imprint of The Templar Company plc,
Pippbrook Mill, London Road, Dorking, Surrey, RH4 1JE, UK
www.templarco.co.uk

ISBN 978-1-84011-567-3

Edited by A. J. Wood

Printed in Italy

Helen Ward

Wonderful Life

Snutt the Ift

or

A Small but Significant Chapter in the Life of the Universe

templar publishing

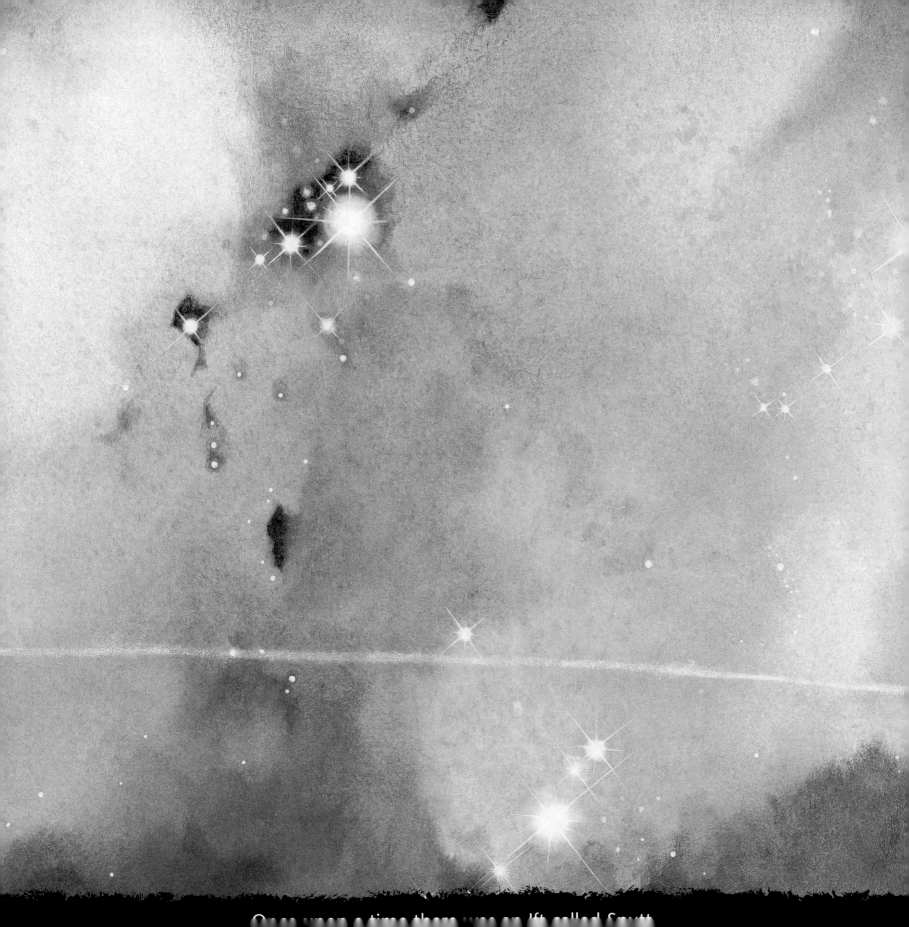

Once upon a time there was an elf called Sprutt.

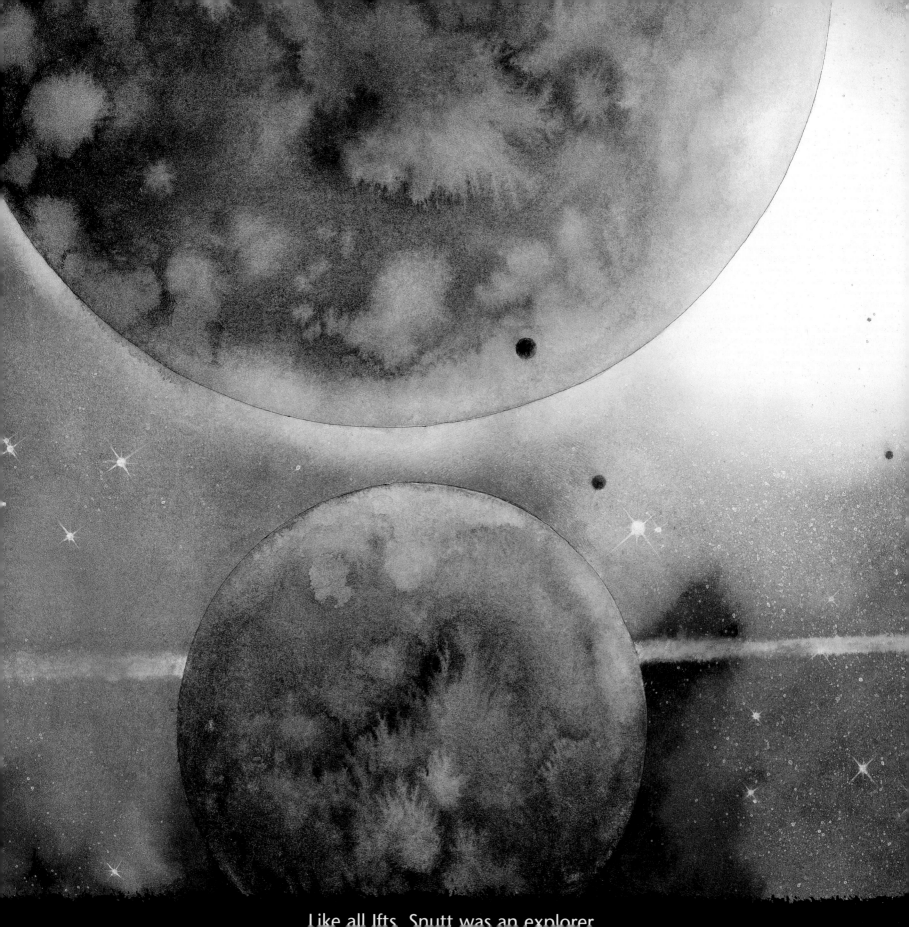

Like all Jfts, Snutt was an explorer.

than any other Ift.

One day, Snutt found a wonderful planet.

A very wonderful planet,

with fields of cheerful tuffetills and delighted blossiblums,

euphoric florifors and sticky-footed flewimols –

too flappy to make the usual notes,

too big to take the usual measurements,

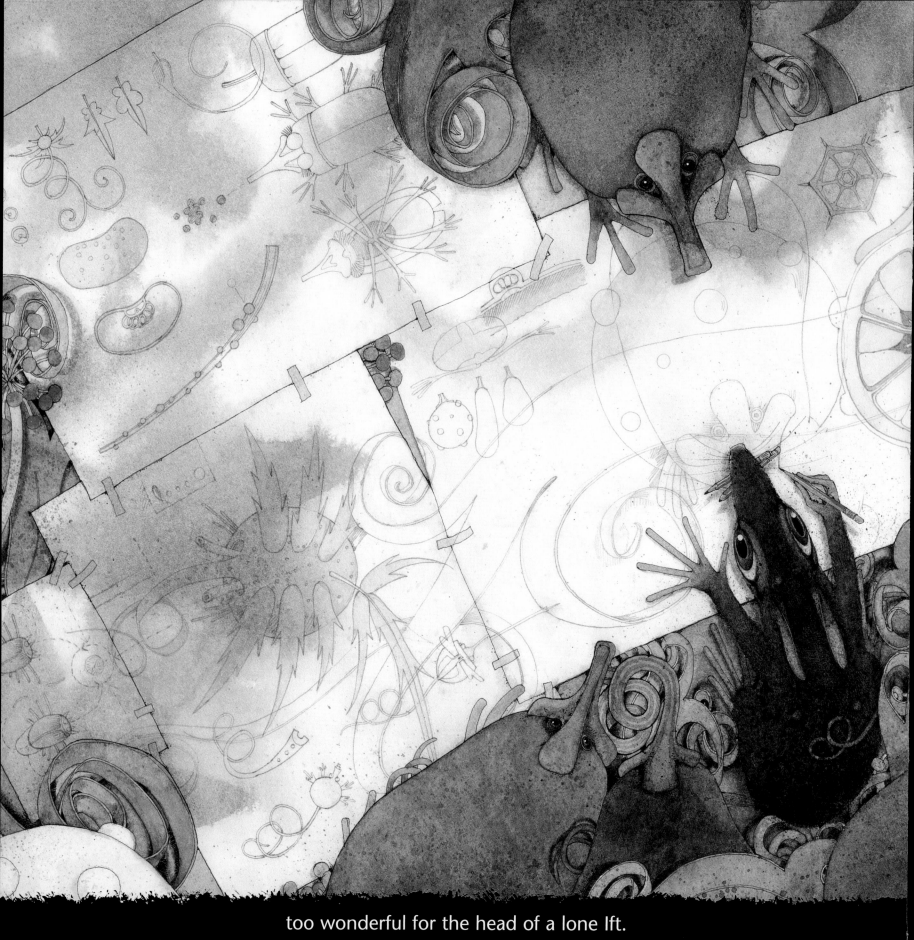

too wonderful for the head of a lone Ift.

and a long, long way from home, Snutt felt very, very lonely.

All the brilliant butterflings…

and fancy flewimols might as well have been dull grey dustmouts,

so, unsurprisingly there were also astonishing coincidences.

There was also a Waft, lost for words and suddenly lonely.

The Ift and the Waft walked in almost the same direction.

through the waving whishgrass. They oooed…

and they aahhed in almost the same way.

They listened and they watched.

And after they had found the very last amazing new thing...

they looked at each other.

Snutt did what all Ifts do when they are very, very happy…

but...

wonderful too...